You will be my baby even when . . .

Christie Becker

Illustrated by
Julie Brayton

You will be my baby even when . . . / Christie Becker; Illustrated by Julie Brayton

C. Becker Books Publishing Company
www.cbeckerbooks.com
cbeckerbooks@yahoo.com

Summary: You will be my baby even when… is a beautiful, heart-warming story that depicts
the transitional stages a parent and child experience throughout their lives together.
The special bond formed between parent and child is strengthened further with each
milestone and will be cherished by both for years to come.

ISBN 0-9728116-0-5
Third Edition

The paintings in this book were done in acrylics.
The display type and text were set in Herbert

Printed and bound in China by Midas Printing International Limited

Dedicated to my babies
Brittany Lauren and Haley Victoria,
my inspirations.

You will be my baby even when you drink from a cup and not from a bottle

and even when
you sleep in a big bed.

and even when
you can dress yourself.

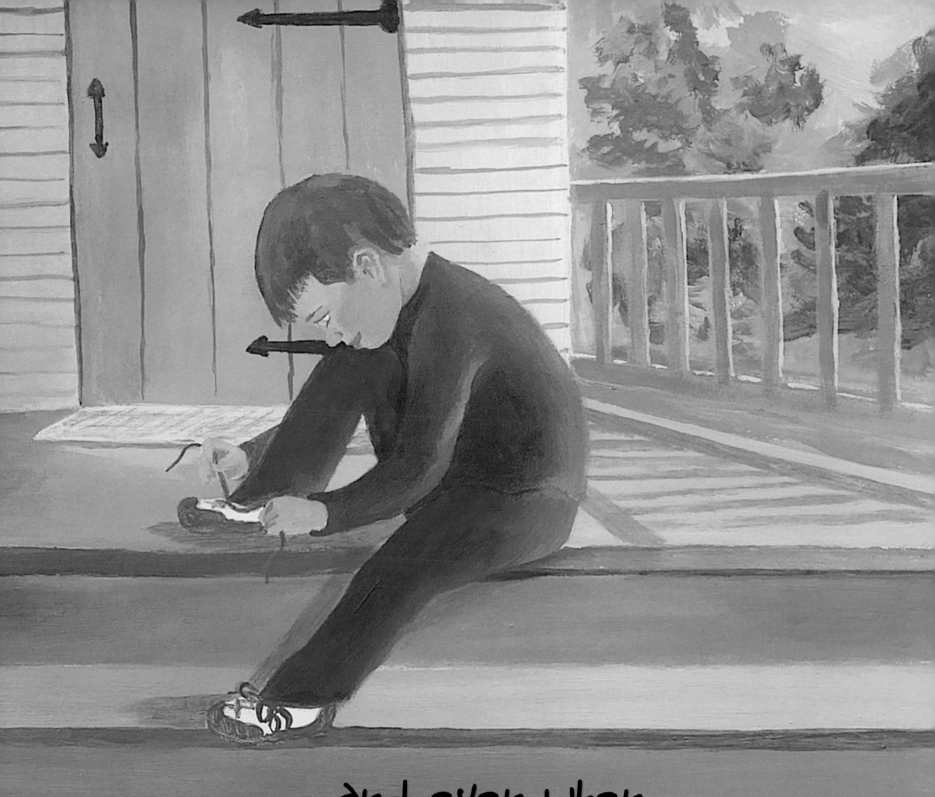

and even when

you can tie your own shoes.

You will be my baby even when you are old enough to drive

and even when
you are taller than me.

and even after
you have a baby of your own.